# THE GIRLS, THE CONVICT

# AND

# THE HIDDEN JEWELS

# THE GIRLS, THE CONVICT AND THE HIDDEN JEWELS

Gia Soni

ZORBA BOOKS

Published by Zorba Books, October 2022

Website: www.zorbabooks.com

Email: info@zorbabooks.com

Author Name & Copyright © Gia Soni

Title: THE GIRLS, THE CONVICT AND THE HIDDEN JEWELS

Printbook ISBN: 978-93-95217-09-5

Ebook ISBN: 978-93-95217-10-1



**Zorba Books Pvt. Ltd. (opc)**
Sushant Arcade,
Next to Courtyard Marriot,
Sushant Lok 1, Gurgaon – 122009, India

Printed by Thomson Press (India) Ltd.

B-315, Okhla Industrial Area, Phase 1, New Delhi- 110020

### Dedicated To

*My Mom who has inspired me to be an author and who has held my hand from a very early age and guided me to be who I am today.*

# CONTENTS

# A NOTE ON THE AUTHOR

Gia is a 10 year old girl who was born and brought up in London. She is a class 5 student at Haberdashers' Girls School. She believes in dreams and the power of magic. Her first word was Mumma and the  second Hippopotamus. She is a voracious reader and loves to read big books and then tries to fantasise about a world that is full of excitement, adventure and magic. She has been writing stories, poems, plays and lots of other stuff for many years now. When she grows up she wants to star in a play in London's West End Theatre that is written by her.

Gia published her 1st book titled 'GIA'S SHORT STORIES' when she was just 6.5 years old. It was launched in Jan 2019 in an event where she shared the stage with a renowned author 'Alan Durant'. This book is a kindle only edition and is available on Amazon: http://bit.ly/giasoni

- Gia was then invited to go on Marlow FM radio talking to Carla Delaney about the inspiration behind her stories

- She was featured in the Asianlite Newspaper for her achievements.

- She was invited to the Houses of Parliament in London in March 2020 and was declared the winner of 'SHE INSPIRES AWARDS-2020' in the 'Bright Artist' category and received the award from Honourable MPs - Virendra Sharma, Padmashree Bob Blackman and Joy Morrissey.

- Gia has been exposed to many charities and decided to donate all earnings through this book to her favourite charity - The Akshaya Patra Foundation UK.

1. Gia's 2nd book THE MYSTERY OF MAGICAL SKETCH PAD was published in June 2021. This book is available on amazon and Flipkart and has won many accolades.

   - Gia was declared the winner of 'SHE INSPIRES AWARDS-2022' in the 'Bright Artist' category in the Houses of Parliament in London.

   - She went live on the Asian Lite radio where she was interviewed on 'How she became an author' of 2 books in March 2022.

   - She won an award in Arts & Culture Category at 'She Awards 2022' event on International Women's day competing against women from all walks of life in the Open Category

   - Gia had a radio interview on how to be an author in December 2021 by AWAZ FM Glasgow.

# ACKNOWLEDGEMENTS

Hi All - Heartfelt thanks to all my readers and well wishers for picking up my book in times when everyone is hooked on to social media.

A sincere and heartfelt thanks to the two strong women in my life - my Nanu, for always persuading me to write stories and my Mum, for always inspiring me to dream big and I owe her big time for becoming an author.

Big hugs to my Daddy, Nana, Mamu and Mami for their constant support and encouragement. Love to my 2 little cousins Aaroo and Mysha who are my biggest cheerleaders.

Wholehearted gratitude towards my teachers at 'Haberdashers' Girls School' for their guidance on the art of storytelling.

This book wouldn't have been possible if I didn't get the right guidance from uncle Rahul Laud and Bhawani Singh Shekhawat. I would like to thank Jose R. Gutierrez for doing the awesome illustrations all the way from venezuela.

A big thanks to my friends for encouraging me to write this 3rd book after I wrote my 1st book when I was just 6.5 years old and 2nd book when I was 8 years old.

Special Thanks to aunty Rashmi Mishra for organising the 'she Inspires Awards -2020 & 2022 ' events in Houses of Parliament, London - where I was recognised for my both books : Gia's Short Stories & The Mystery of Magical Sketch Pad.

With that, it's time for 'another adventure and being part of the stormier world of Suzie, Lily and Annie…

# CHAPTER 1

# SCHOOL'S OUT!

It was the last day of school before the summer holidays started and none of the pupils could focus on their work. Their substitute teacher, Mrs Smith, had been called in today because their geography tutor had fallen ill. Today was not a good day for Mrs Smith. The excitement of the upcoming holiday was rushing through everyone's veins because it was only one hour until school finished! Mrs Smith was doing a geography quiz but none of the students were focused on her. How could they be, with only sixty minutes until school ended for the summer? The lesson went by with irritating slowness and with poor Mrs Smith trying to teach a class of uninterested students and nobody listening to her. Eventually, it was one minute until school was over for the semester and everybody was buzzing with anticipation. School should be finished any moment now.

And then she heard it… The sweetest sound in the world, like a thousand harmonious melodies playing with the strings of her heart, Annie finally heard the bell signalling the end of school. In a few seconds, there were students pouring out onto the corridors, talking to their friends about their plans for the summer. As soon as school had ended, the girls all went to Lily and Suzie's house and had a big water fight. It was a silly tradition that every year, they would take their pistols and guns out and would squirt each other. After that, they would have a barbecue and an entertaining sleepover. For them, that was the thing that would excite them all and would get the girls into the festive, holiday mood. Last year, Caroline had taken a photo of the sleepover in action and Suzie, Lily and Annie had framed a copy of it on their bedroom walls.

After that, the girls had a ball of a time playing, chatting and going to the shops to buy sweets. While Lily was doing her homework the previous night, she found out that on July the 7th, National Macaroni day was celebrated. And, since it was the 7th of July, they decided to make some scrumptious Mac'n Cheese to celebrate it. However, despite their best efforts, they couldn't get the dish to taste just right. After a couple of failed attempts, they gave up and decided to order some from a local Italian place just down the road.

# CHAPTER 2

# FUN IN ITALY !

As well as Suzie and Lily's family, Annie's family had come to Sorrento for a fun holiday together, due to the girls' incessant nagging. The mums had told the girls to be back at their luxury hotel at noon, but up till then, the children could go wherever they wanted. "We should go to a nice restaurant as Italy always has the best food - pizza and pasta! What's not to love?" Lily exclaimed brightly. Annie countered, "Actually, even though I agree with you, we should go to the beach. The water is usually freezing in England but now that we're here in Italy, it's really nice and warm!"

The girls decided to head to the beach, hoping to get a light snack on the way. The salty sea ocean was an azure, serene body of water and the relaxing sound of the waves lapping against the glistening, golden sand pacified all of the girls' thoughts. They got sunburnt and enjoyed a relaxing time at the beach while they sipped on some refreshing ice tea. The merry music playing in the background was so jolly that it made the girls want to dance along to the jovial tune. The sun had become a burning ball of flames in the blissful sky as it looked down at all of the sun-kissed children playing about in the sand.

"Shall we swim in the sea or will we just be lazing about on the sand?" Annie asked impatiently. The girls went and had a lot of fun while splashing each other, jumping over waves and seeing schools of fish swim by. However, that was not the best part of the morning. It was when they went out to have ice cream, or gelato as you called it in Italy, the shop was supposed to have the freshest and most delicious gelato in the whole world! Suzie had a strawberry flavoured ice cream with a flake in it; Lily had hazelnut ice cream with sprinkles and Annie took such a long time deciding her flavour that Lily and Suzie's cones were dripping by the time she finally ordered. "Pistachio looks good but I also think that limone looks nice too!" she exclaimed. After very careful thinking, Annie established that the Pistachio flavour was a must - have and had that along with a chocolate covered cone.

The families were reunited at the hotel and they all went back to their hotel. It was an extravagant place to stay in and that made the girls feel like proper ladies while staying there. There was a mocktail and cocktail bar, an infinity swimming pool and rooms with the best views in all of the Amalfi Coast. Their balconies overlooked jagged cliffs and the turquoise ocean. The families ate AntiPasti and chatted happily while drinking freshly squeezed orange juice. This holiday was turning out to be the most exciting by far and everything seemed too good to be true. Suzie thought that life could not possibly be any better, but it just became nicer when they found out that there was a surprise trip planned to go to a water park. But it was not just any water park, it was the one with the longest slide in the country! There were more slides in that park than the girls had ever seen before and there was nothing that they would rather do.

# CHAPTER 3

# PASTA GALORE !

Roaming around Sorrento, while the children were off having fun, the adults were having a great deal of pleasure tasting different local cuisines and they were even given a special experience. David had booked a tour around a pasta making factory and would be seeing all of the steps and the recipes. It was such a big deal because of the fact that nobody else was offered this wonderful opportunity. The only reason David had been able to book this amazing chance was because Papa Joe had known the manager of the factory and he had pulled a few strings. "A friend of Joe is a friend of mine." The jolly manager exclaimed. That was why the girls had to meet the adults at noon - the tour was at 12:30 and so there would be no time to waste. No one had been aware of this and it was a surprise to everybody. They saw how bolognese sauce was made and saw how the pasta was just made from flour and then was put into a special machine which could sculpt it into different shapes.

"Can we buy a pasta machine daddy? Pretty please with a cherry on top" Lily pleaded with puppy eyes. David replied while chuckling, "Maybe, but let's pay attention to the actual pasta making now. If you're good then I'll think about it". Lily straightened up and was helping at every possible opportunity from then on. "Did you know that the sauce in a linguine is called Alfredo?" The manager asked in a thick accent. The tour took one and a half hours and by the time it was finished, everyone was looking desperate to try the freshly made pasta and have something to eat. Throughout the tour, they were only allowed to eat little bits and bobs and it was practically impossible to not be tempted by the sweet aroma of the freshly baked pasta. Their hunger was finally satiated by the most tasty buttered ravioli filled with ricotta and spinach.

However, you know what happens when you're having fun… Time flew by like seconds and everyone, adults and children, dreaded the unfortunate time when their lovely holiday would come to an end. Lily begged to be able to stay back in Italy but Caroline had made it clear that it wasn't a choice. The flight felt long and tiring but the girls watched movies the whole time, while the adults slept - preparing themselves for their arrival to England. Upon coming back to London, the gloomy weather just reminded the girls of their amazing trip and how it was over. However, when the sun came out from its hiding place behind the clouds, grins crawled from the edges of their mouths. Unfortunately, the next day, they found that something terrible had happened…

# CHAPTER 4

# HAVOC EVERYWHERE !

"No!" Suzie cried as she scoured her room for the sketchpad. "Where is it? It has to be here somewhere!" In a distressed state of mind, Suzie was frantically hurling clothes across the room while desperately searching for the sketchpad. She had looked under her bed, emptied all of her drawers and looked through every single book on her shelf. It wasn't there. What was she going to do? She tidied up the giant mess and with a surrendering sigh, she turned to the door, and in the corner of her eye, through the window, she saw a hooded figure clutching a thick book. Could this be her sketchpad and if so, why were they taking it? If this mysterious person had indeed stolen their sketchpad, they would be very sorry that they did. She would make sure of it herself.

She slid down the banister and was about to enter the garden when she came to an abrupt halt. Up until a few days ago, their garden had been neglected and had become a mess of overgrown weeds. But since the gardener had done some work on it, as she pushed her way through the lush grass she could see that it was now a delightful, emerald green paradise! There were scarlett roses everywhere and the grass had been cut down to just the right height - and that was just the flora! There were buzzing honeybees busily darting around collecting nectar and there was euphorious music that was created and composed by crickets eagerly chirping. This lifted Suzie's mood and she momentarily forgot to tell Lily and Annie about what she had seen. She snapped out of it when her dad rushed up to her and told her to do the laundry. She began protesting but then hesitated as knew there was no option because of a look that told her 'Suzie you have no option but to listen to me'. She lost ten valuable minutes while doing her chores and was unsure if they could possibly find the thief with all of the lost time, but still she carried on in a hurry.

Bursting into the cosy, wooden shed, panting like a tired puppy, Suzie explained all that she had seen in as few words possible, "Sketchpad… stolen… girl in a hoodie, laundryyyyy!" Annie jumped to the ceiling in surprise and Lily was so astounded that she looked like she had eaten a red chilli for the very first time. Anxiously, the girls sprinted to the door to check whether the thief was still there but no one was to be seen outside. Annie instinctively began looking for any clues that would lead them to the intruder. She found small dirt footprints and bike tracks near the pavement. Would an experienced burglar leave so recklessly, why were the footprints so small, why would anyone want to steal the sketchpad? Nobody knew that it had magical powers and gave clues to solve real life problems.

There was no time to think though, and the girls began to follow the trail and they were in utter shock when the prints led in the direction of a broken-down shack. Lily was prepared to storm into the shack and demand the sketchpad back, but in the end they agreed that they should wait and come up with a well thought plan. The minutes went by like seconds as the girls brainstormed until they had an idea that everyone was happy with. Their plan was to sneak into the shack when no one was there, search for the sketchpad and steal it back.

# CHAPTER 5

## THE PLAN

"What if they catch us? What happens if they have alarms?" Suzie asked worriedly. Once the other girls assured her that everything would be okay, which took quite a long time, they decided that they would meet at Papa Joe's Pizzeria on Sunday morning. This was mainly because their parents would be asleep until late in the morning and they could go and come back without anyone noticing. The plan seemed perfect and the girls were immensely ecstatic until something terrible happened…

On Saturday night, there were weather warnings for the next day. At first, the girls took absolutely no notice of what the warnings said until a horrendous storm came along on Sunday morning. Thunder boomed, lightning lit up the jet black sky, torrential rain pounded on the roofs of all buildings and hard raindrops hit the faces of anyone who dared to stick their head outside for even a millisecond. Humongous chunks of debris and fallen trees were whipping the wooden doors, threatening to enter the houses of every little cottage in town.

Annie phoned Suzie and Lily, "Hey guys, we really need to talk about our plan and the weather." she said, sounding as deflated as a balloon.

Dejected Lily answered in a very solemn way, "Oh dear! What are we going to do? What if the robber has given it to someone or has thrown it away? When will we get our sketchpad back?"

Suzie spoke in a melancholy voice which added to the depression, "Yeah, but we simply can't go in this weather. We probably should have paid more attention to the weather warning yesterday." After coming from Italy, the girls knew that not everything would be as amazing as it was there but nobody had thought that things would go this downhill.

"Well if we can't go out today then we'll have to make another plan - I'm going for a sleepover at my Aunt's house tomorrow." Annie muttered in clear anguish, " I hope nothing's happened to our sketchpad." The girls were in distress for the rest of the day and had settled into their desperate mood as the clouds grew grey and relentless hailstones banged against the roof. "It's supposed to be spring with flowers and blossoms springing out from the ground. It's winter all over again!" Lily moaned with her head in her hands. Thankfully, the rain stopped the next day and people started to come out of their damaged houses once more.

# CHAPTER 6

# CAN WE TRUST HER ?

The girls decided that they would put their plan into action on the same day and decided to go to the robber's 'house' (if you could call it one). At 10am, Annie, Suzie and Lily were dashing through the streets, excited for the oncoming adventure. Once they reached the shack, the girls wondered whether they should barge in or wait until they were sure that the house was empty.

In the end, they waited behind a bush for about 15 minutes before Suzie got impatient and started walking up to the wooden door. At that moment, she was going to knock on the door, but a young girl, who was about their age, walked out and almost collided with unsuspecting Suzie. The poor girl looked frightened out of her wits and ran back to the safety of her home. However, by that time, Annie had sprung from her hiding place and caught hold of the girl's hand. "Who are you? I saw you steal my sketchpad!" Annie demanded in an interrogative way. "It's actually our sketchpad," Lily butted in, "but you get the point." The girl blurted out, "I'm sorry, my uncle made me do that - it's not my fault. I'll answer all of your questions but please come in. I don't want anyone to be suspicious" and with that, she held the door open. She was brushing hair out of her face and was looking solemnly down at the ground.

After she knew that she could relax a bit, Suzie had more time to look at the girl's features. She had light brown hair that came down in gentle waves. Her pale skin tone suggested that she was apprehensive and all of the colour in her cheeks had flooded away. The girl explained,"I'm Zara and I live with my uncle - Robert. He's an archaeologist and is working with a colleague who isn't that nice, but it's not like my uncle's nice either. He forced me to steal your book and he said that if I didn't, he would throw me out of the house and onto the street. You see, he was in Papa Joe's pizzeria and he heard Papa Joe muttering something about some magical sketchpad in your house. He made me steal it because he wanted to sell it at a private auction. So far, none of the buyers believe that it's magic so none of them want to buy it. I'm really sorry but I didn't have much of a choice. Here you can have it back as it's of no use to my uncle anymore" she explained, looking down at the floor.

# CHAPTER 7

# MYSTERY UNCOVERED!

"Oh my gosh, he sounds so mean!" Annie responded, deep in thought, "I wonder who would want to buy it in the first place." At the same time, Lily whispered to Suzie, "How do we know we can actually trust her? She's still just a stranger who we've never met before." Suzie responded with a threatening glare. Zara did look like she was genuinely frightened but Lily was right, this girl had stolen their sketchpad after all, she might just be deceiving them. Annie said, "Don't worry, we now know that it wasn't your fault after all. But, we'll do some investigating anyway to get to the bottom of this. We know the sketchpad's powers and if your uncle wanted it, it couldn't have been for something good." Her talk was met by nods and murmurs of "Yeah, totally." A gasp was drawn by Annie as she thought of a brilliant idea, "Let me take your number, and I'll call you and stay on mute and if you hide your phone somewhere inconspicuous, we'll be able to watch and hear what your uncle's plotting." Lily looked absolutely excited at the thought of something so interesting to do,"Let's do it! What a great idea!" The girls exchanged phone numbers and once the plan had been finalised, the children were super excited to see what the future held in stock for them. Would this lead to a great big find or would it only lead to another dead end? Only time would tell...

Annie, Suzie and Lily were all at Annie's house for another sleepover and they were now watching and listening to Zara and her uncle - incognito. They could glimpse a door creaking open and could hear a brusque voice asking, "Zara, did you return that useless book?" "Yes uncle," Zara replied, "I'm feeling a little sleepy so I might go to bed now." The voice replied,"Sure." Zara faced the camera (which was hidden amongst the crack between the wall and her bed) and winked and then pretended to snore. Five minutes later, her uncle came into view - he was a large, plump man and after looking at him, you couldn't help but wonder what he ate that made him so enormous. He sat on a little, wooden stool and greedily grabbed the landline phone and typed in a number. The conversation was not too clear but the girls could just about follow along. It went something like this, "Yeah yeah, I'll be there on Friday. Don't be late, Oliver J will come by the time we've started, and I don't wish to see him. Bring the money in cash, I'm selling it to you for quite a good price. Understood? Good good. See you then".

Suzie then hung up the call, while Annie was eagerly writing notes on a notebook that she had grabbed from one of her shelves. "We have so much to do and Friday, that's only in 6 days. We've got to get busy. If it's something big then we'll have to report it a day before so that the police can get themselves ready. "When can we start investigating?" Lily asked earnestly. The girls decided that they would have to go to sleep now, as it had almost reached midnight. The next day, in the hopes for a new adventure, The girls woke up with buzzing ideas of where to start. Working together as a group, the children persuaded their parents to allow them to go over to Suzie and Lily's house. At noon, everybody was settled and the girls were brainstorming ideas on what to do next.

# CHAPTER 8

## WHO'S OLIVER?

The words 'Oliver J' had been running in the girls' heads all morning. None of them had ever heard of him, but, if they were to find out, then they would have to go to the post office and request the phone book and somehow find him in the book. He had to be a key part of the mystery, right? Reaching the post office had been surprisingly easy as the girls got their bikes and rode down the road. The lady at the post office however, had been wary of giving the phone book to children (as she should have been) but in the end, after convincing the lady at the counter, the girls were given the book. Except she had insisted that she supervised them to make sure that they wouldn't get up to any mischief. They did find an Oliver Jack - but only after thoroughly going through about two hundred names

and, to their surprise, it was underlined in red. Out of curiosity, Lily questioned why the name had been marked. The lady answered, "That means that the person has a criminal record," she angled the book towards herself, "oh this is Oliver, he got out of prison a while ago, he lives just behind the pub over there." she pointed to a little pub across the street. Upon hearing this, Annie went as scarlet as a tomato, "So we're dealing with someone who has been in jail? OMG, this is going to be a lot more challenging than I thought." Lily, Suzie and Annie finalised a plan while walking home from the post office. The girls would meet the next day and find out more about who this 'Oliver Jack' was and what he was planning to do on Thursday.

The next day, the girls were hyper energetic all morning and were eager to find Oliver's house. There were not many houses on the road behind the pub. The girls slowly walked on the road and came across a strangely tattered house. Upon seeing his house, the girls were immediately able to tell that it was old, really old. There was ivy growing up the side of the house and the bricks were slowly crumbling away. However, the thing that most surprised Suzie was the large amount of flowers. There wasn't one speck of grass that hadn't been used up for gardening. "Wow, this looks lovely and quaint." Annie exclaimed while admiring a Rhododendron bush with crimson bulbs. Lily, eager to get going, replied, "Come on, we don't have much time, let's see what this 'Oliver Jack' has to say." They opened the creaky gate with its paint peeling away and treaded lightly, trying not to step on the rows of flowerbeds and Suzie rapped on the front door. And there it was - a plaque that had the name 'Oliver Jack' on it. However, there was no reply...

# CHAPTER 9

# FINDING OUT MORE

Annie got bored of waiting as she always did and knocked harder and to her surprise, found that the door was open. They looked at each other and decided to creeped in, trying not to be heard as Lily whispered something about how they could get arrested for breaking in. Should they be doing this? Earlier, Suzie had convinced herself that this was just helping Zara out, but was it right? Had somebody been there, they would have been caught as Annie was being clumsy and had walked into a wall three times. Eventually, Lily and Annie decided to have a quick glance around the house, while Suzie looked outside the window for signs of activity. They found a diary on the bedside table and read through some of the first few pages. "Oh my goodness! You won't believe this but a Robert is mentioned in here. It has to be Zara's uncle." Suzie exclaimed in joy. The girls then hastily went through the rest of the beautifully calligraphed pages.

On the last page, there was a set of coordinates. Annie texted the coordinates onto her phone and was shocked to find that they lead to an isolated section of the beach south of the pier. Just then, Suzie saw a car pull into the pebbly driveway. That was when they decided to leave and then they sprinted as rapidly as the wind. It was a narrow escape but the girls managed to get out of what could have been a very tricky situation. In the afternoon, the girls met up at Annie's house and they talked about the pages they had read earlier. The girls had found out that Oliver and Robert had been partners in crime until Oliver got arrested and somehow, Robert didn't. After that, he had no contact with Robert ever again. "No wonder that Robert doesn't want to meet Oliver as they don't exactly have the best history." Suzie said happily, glad that things were starting to make more sense now.

"Well that's a great find but we still need to go there again to check why he's going to the beach on Thursday. Who knows when he wrote those coordinates? For now, that's the only clue we can work with." Suzie said dejectedly. However, she cheered up after they went out for ice lollies. Annie got a twister, Suzie got a Coca Cola calippo and Lily ordered a nobbly bobbly. The mystery was still fresh in their minds the next day when the girls took Roger out for a walk. "Hey, let's try to speak to Oliver, we only have 3 more days now." Lily spoke in a hushed voice so that no attention was drawn to them. This time, they were a little bit more lucky - Oliver was in the house as the girls knocked on the door for the second time. As they had been thinking a lot about the unending puzzle, it had been fairly easy to make up a cover story.

"Hi Mr. Oliver, in class, we've been asked to research a bit about an eco-friendly person. And because of the amount of flowers in your garden, we thought that you would be the perfect candidate." Annie said. If Oliver was feeling bewildered as to why there were three strangers on his doorstep, he hid it very well. From the beginning, the girls seemed very confident in their pretend roles and were busy asking questions to Oliver. In the end, they managed to extract just about enough information to confirm that he would be going to the beach that day - somewhere south of the pier and it was a place of 'special importance' to him. He refused to say any more except for the fact that the place was connected with his past. The girls left his place and Lily couldn't contain her enthusiasm, "Connected with his past? It has to be about Zara's uncle, it just has to!". Now that they were sure about the when and where, they had decided to wait until after lunch to take more action. Until then, the mystery would unfold as scheduled.

# CHAPTER 10

# THE SECLUDED BEACH!

"We need to be quick now Lily, Suzie said, "We need to go and come back before anyone notices that we're gone, otherwise, our parents will never stop asking us questions about where we went, why we went etc." Suzie spoke quietly, so that she didn't alert anyone. The girls met up in the afternoon and decided to explore this place where the mysterious event would take place. They had to take a train and then walk a fair bit to go to the exact place that the coordinates pointed to. "Oh my gosh, it's so far away. No way am I walking here again!" Lily complained, "Although, it is quite tucked away - this is the perfect place to do secret things." Annie quickly corrected her, "Secret, Illegal things, not just any secret things." That shut Lily up straightaway.

After reaching the place, the girls first checked that no one was there and then they explored the area for clues. Annie found a wooden crate tucked behind a huge mound of sand and looked inside the crate after calling Suzie and Lily. "Wow, jackpot! I think this is part of an old ship." Annie exclaimed excitedly. Lily replied sarcastically, "Wow there's a ship. Hip hip hooray, all of our problems are solved." Upon hearing that, Annie spoke in an exasperated voice, "No, I mean a really old ship. Like from the viking times!"

Hearing that made Lily go absolutely crazy with excitement. Upon closer examination, the girls noticed that the ship's parts still had some mud on them. Suzie, who was speaking aloud said,

"Hey, Zara's uncle - he was an architect - he probably found this after digging somewhere. But why would he be hiding this? It's amazing!"

Then suddenly they could hear people's voices coming towards their direction and the girls hid behind a mound of sand. The conversation happened a little far away so the girls couldn't hear everything, but they could just about follow along. However they did recognise Robert in the distance and heard something along the lines, " Need to sell... potential buyers, hurry! Oliver... coming tomorrow. He'll find out." The girls stayed still for what seemed like an eternity and after making sure that Robert had gone, the girls headed back home in silence. What were they supposed to do? Something was scheduled to happen in two days and they had no idea of what to do - so they finally agreed to do the only thing they could think of.

# CHAPTER 11

# WHAT WILL HAPPEN NEXT?

They called the chief of police and told her everything that they knew. The officer's name was Lana, "So you're telling me that there's a ship that's on the old beach by the pier that we, the police force, don't know about?" she asked dubiously, " We're not blind you know." In the end, the girls couldn't manage to persuade Lana to even take a look at the ship and it was clear that she didn't believe them. After a lot of deep thought, Annie spoke in a small voice, "Well, I guess we're alone on this one.

The next day, the girls went back to the seashore and looked at the ancient ship (or what was left of it at least) and made a truly astounding discovery. Lily had peeked through one of the windows and saw five barrels full of something - they were jewels! There were sapphires, emeralds, rubies, amethysts and diamonds, all glinting in the sunlight. The girls were shivering in excitement and thought about this for long and still could not come up with a plan. Annie reached into her pocket to take out her phone and click a photo of the jewels but to her dismay, she realised that she had left it at home. They knew that the police wouldn't believe them and so they rushed back home and bursted through Annie's front door. They decided to tell Annie's dad who used to be a policeman. At first he thought that they were joking but when he realised that they were not, he got much more serious. "You're telling me that there's a ship with treasure inside of it? Like a pirate treasure?" He asked questionably.

Nevertheless, James, who was Annie's father, went to have a look at the ship and was blown away. In all his years of being a cop, he had never seen anything more mind blowing and stunning than this. He called the police and as he was an adult, they decided to check whether what he was saying was true. "Oh and this whole selling the goods thing is supposed to be happening tomorrow, so yeah, I just thought you should know." Lily added in while they were waiting for the police. James put his head in his hands and groaned, "Gosh, Lily. Couldn't you have mentioned this a little earlier?" Knowing that the buyers would be coming tomorrow made everyone much more pressured than they already were. All of the preparations and arrangements would have to be made in one night.

As the police arrived, it was all a blur: everything was happening so fast and Lily couldn't make sense of it all. Lana had walked up to them and had apologised profoundly to the girls for not believing them,"I really am sorry. I still can't believe that they were trying to smuggle jewels and we had no idea about it." she said for what seemed like the hundredth time before walking away. The police had decided to catch them red-handed while they were trying to sell the ship and then they would arrest Robert for treating Zara so badly. Since the girls had helped them immensely, the cops had allowed them to watch the whole heist, but only from far keeping their safety in mind.

It was Thursday, the day when everything was going to really come into action. Would they catch hold of Robert and his friend? Or would it all go to waste? The girls met at Papa Joe's Pizzeria and grabbed a pepperoni pizza to go while they waited at the seaside (the whole crime could take a long time as Lily said). At first, things went really slowly but then Zara's uncle came along with the potential buyer and started to move the jewels. At that moment, the police sprang out like a cat on a chase and arrested both of them.

The victory of the arrest felt even better to the children because they knew that they had played a vital part in it. A short while after that, Oliver Jack came walking by and was very surprised to see the whole area covered by police tape with writing saying 'POLICE - do not enter'. He wondered what had been happening there but he simply walked past it without stopping to have a second glance.

One of Zara's relatives had volunteered to take her in and was utterly disgusted to find out how badly Zara had been treated. Zara was very grateful to the girls for being such good people and for looking after her so well. Annie, Suzie and Lily remained in touch with her for a long time afterwards and they met each other frequently for playdates. The girls were regarded as local heroes from that time onwards and the police department thought that Lily, Annie and Suzie had been extremely brave and courageous in solving the mystery. To honour that, Lara gave them a little trophy to keep. They had a mini ceremony with biscuits and hot chocolate, but most of the time, they were just asked to repeat the story and what had happened.

"I'm so glad that now we can just relax and live like normal people, not having to worry about anything, especially somebody trying to steal your belongings." Suzie exclaimed cheerfully. Annie retaliated, "Are you kidding me? It's been so much fun solving the mystery and finding out stuff from clues!" While muttering under her breath, Suzie replied, "Yeah, I guess." Lily said, "I think we should just get on with the rest of our summer. It'll be over before we even realise it."

www.ingramcontent.com/pod-product-compliance
Lightning Source LLC
LaVergne TN
LVHW051514170726
843492LV00002B/927